The mystery of the buried treasure

My cousin had moved to a new house and I had gone over to help him and his family to move in. Gary was the same age as me and so we got on well. 'When we have finished lifting in the boxes, I want to show you something strange that I found in the garden,' Gary said 'What do you mean by strange?'
'You will see,' he said.

After a couple of hours of helping with the boxes, Gary's dad thanked me. He also said that Gary and I could go and play. We grabbed an apple each and went out into the garden. 'Over here,' called Gary. 'Come and have a look'.
He led the way to the back of the garden near the fence. 'What do you make of that?'

Gary pointed to a square shaped lid made of concrete about the size of a folded newspaper. It was set into the ground. It was partly covered with leaves and soil. We brushed away the leaves to get a better look at it. There was a metal ring set into one end of the concrete lid. 'A trap door to a hidden room, maybe?' I said. 'Or maybe to a ladder leading down into a cave?'

'Too small I think as an entrance to anything,' Gary replied. 'I think that it's a lid to something. Let's try and lift it up with that ring.'
Gary hooked his fingers through the ring and gave it a tug. Nothing happened. The concrete looked really heavy and seemed to be stuck down well.
'Let me help.' I reached down and tried to pull up the side of the slab while Gary pulled at the ring. But it was still no good.

'Hey, there must be some tools in your garage,'
I said to Gary. 'We could use a crowbar and a
spade and see if we could lift it up.'
'Good idea. And I'll ask my dad if he can give
us a hand as well.'
'What do you think is under there?'
'I don't know. But someone really wanted to
keep it safe I guess.'

We told Gary's dad about what we had found and he came with us to get the tools. 'You have to be careful when you find something like this,' Gary's dad said. 'Sometimes the companies that run the electricity lines and the water pipes have doorways like this which only they can use. You shouldn't touch those at all as it could be dangerous.' We came to the spot and Gary's dad bent down to look at the concrete. 'But if that was the case they would have their name and symbol printed on the concrete. So I think this is something else. Let's see what we can find.'

'Here, you boys tie this rope to the ring and
loop the other end of it over that branch. Then
when I tell you, both of you pull on the rope
with all your strength. I'll use the crowbar at the
same time and we will see if we can pull it up,'
said Gary's dad.

Gary's dad got the crowbar into position and then he called out, 'Pull!' Gary and I pulled on the rope. But nothing happened.
'Try it again!' Again we pulled. Suddenly there was a clunking sound and Gary and I fell down on the grass as the concrete lifted up.
'That's it!' called Gary's dad. 'Well done, boys!' We raced across to look into the hole. 'Well, how about that,' said Gary's dad as he reached into the hole. 'I think it's a time capsule.'

'A time capsule? What's that?' I bent forward to
see what he had put on the grass. It looked like
a piece of steel pipe. It was closed at one end
and had a sort of lid at the other end. It was
very rusty.

'A time capsule is a special container that people sometimes hide for other people to find years later. Inside it they may put a copy of a newspaper, some coins, perhaps a photo of the people who put the capsule and even a note. In a way, it's like sending a message to people of the future. This one might have been put here by the people who used to live in this house I guess or maybe the people before them. Let's have a look inside.'

13

Gary's dad gave the lid of the capsule a hit
with the crowbar and then slowly unscrewed it.
He then tipped the capsule so that its contents
spilled out on to the grass.
'Wow!' cried out Gary. 'It's just like you said!
Look at that old stuff!'
It was great! There were coins, a photo of the
house taken long time ago, some postage
stamps, the front page of a newspaper and
lastly an envelope.

Gary's dad opened the envelope. He read the letter out to us. 'To whoever finds this, we send you a message from the past. We are writing this in the year 1940 and . . .,' the letter read. The letter went on to tell us about the people who had lived there and what they did and about their family and what was happening in the world at that time. Gary and I thought that it was wonderful. We have put the treasures from the time capsule into a special box in his bedroom so that we can look at them again from time to time.

Now we're putting together a new time capsule to go into the same hole, and we're writing a letter that will go in it, to the people of the future.

What is that noise?

'What is that noise?' I wondered. It was a low rumbling sound followed by a sort of whoosh. I turned on the bedside light to see if I could see what was making that noise.

It was Sandra. Sandra is my best friend and she was staying the night at our house. The school holidays were going on. We had been talking in bed for ages and now Sandra was snoring! I turned off the light and gave Sandra's arm a gentle push to make her roll over a bit, which made her stop snoring. That was better.

wap - wap · wap . . .

I was nearly asleep when I heard a strange
wap-wap-wap noise. 'What is it this time,' I
thought. I listened for a little while trying to think
what it might be. It wasn't a scary sound at all!
But I knew that I wouldn't sleep until I found out
what it was.

I opened the window and listened. There it was
again. I peered into the dark. Ah, now I could
see that it was the cat from the next door trying
to open the lid of the rubbish bin. I screwed up
a bit of paper and threw it at the cat. She ran
away. Maybe, I would sleep now.

But I was not lucky enough I guess.
'Zzzzzzzzzzzzz, Zzzzzzzzzz.' There was a
mosquito right beside my ear! I waved my
hands at it but it kept coming back. I turned the
light on. There it was, on the wall. I took a rolled
up magazine and squashed it.

Sandra woke up. 'What's going on? Why are you making so much noise?' I turned off the light and settled down into the blankets.

I yawned. I was really very tired by now. I felt that I could sleep for hours and hours. I was really looking forward to sleep, and maybe some nice dreams.

'Thump! Thump!' The neighbours had arrived home from the movies. They were banging the car's doors and talking loudly about the movie they had seen. Finally, they went inside.

I was glad that we had holidays in school. If the next day would have been working, I wouldn't be of much use. I looked at the clock. I could see the numbers on the face of the clock. It was 11.30. Please let it be quiet now!

Just then, the front door crashed open and my big brother and two of his friends came from the party. A few seconds later they played loud music. Oh no! Then I heard dad ask them to turn the music down a bit but it was still keeping me awake. I put my head under the pillow.

The next moment blue and red lights lit up
the room. A police car and a fire engine
were racing down our street. 'Wheeowww!
Wheeowww!' went their sirens.

Now the clock showed 12.30. It was past midnight!
I lay there with my eyes open for a few minutes and
then I must have fallen asleep.

The next thing I knew was that it was morning.
The sun was up and Sandra was shaking my
arm. 'Hey, wake up!'
'What's going on?' I asked sitting up in bed.
'It's such a nice morning! I thought we should
get up early and play outside. What's wrong?
You look very tired.' 'Oh well, maybe tonight I'll
be able to sleep properly,' I thought.

New words

anything	entrance	metal	snore
apple	envelope	mosquito	soil
beat	finally	movie	spade
bedside	finger	name	square
blanket	finish	neighbour	squash
box	fire engine	note	steel
branch	fold	partly	strength
brush	forward	people	symbol
bury	future	photo	thank
careful	garage	piece	time capsule
cave	glad	pillow	tipped
clunk	grab	pipe	tool
coin	hatch	police	trap door
company	hide	postage stamp	treasure
concrete	hook	reach	tug
container	hour	ring	turn off
content	ladder	roll	unscrew
cousin	lead	room	wave
cover	lid	rubbish bin	yawn
crash	lift	rumble	
crowbar	line	safe	
danger	loud	settle down	
dream	magazine	siren	
electricity	message		

What did you learn?

The mystery of the buried treasure

How did the boys and Gary's father lift up the hatch?

What was inside the time capsule?

In what year was the letter written?

What is that noise?

What noise did Sandra make when she fell asleep?

What made the noise Zzzzzzzzzzzzzzz?

What time did the girl finally go to sleep?